Dachy's
Deaf

First published in 2012 by Wayland
Text and illustrations © Jack Hughes 2012

Wayland
338 Euston Road
London NW1 3BH

Wayland Australia
Level 17/207 Ken t Street
Sydney, NSW 2000

Editor: Victoria Brooker
Design: Lisa Peacock and Steve Prosser

British Library Cataloguing in Publication Data
Hughes, Jack.
Dachy's deaf. -- (The dinosaur friends)
1. Deafness--Pictorial works--Juvenile fiction.
2. Children's stories--Pictorial works.
I. Title II. Series
823.9'2-dc23

ISBN 978 0 7502 7056 4
Printed in China

Wayland is a division of Hachette Children's Books,
an Hachette UK Company
www.hachette.co.uk

Dachy's Deaf

Written and illustrated by Jack Hughes

WAYLAND

BUZZZZZZZZZ!

Dachy wore a hearing aid. With his hearing aid, Dachy could hear many sounds. BUZZZZZZZZZZ! The gentle buzzing sound of a busy bumblebee.

TWEET, TWEET, TWEET! The sound of a bird singing high above. SWISH, SWISH, SWISH! The sound the wind makes as it gently blows through the trees.

TWEET! TWEET! TWEET!

However, when Dachy's hearing aid was switched off, he could hear very little at all.

Sometimes Dachy's friends were far too noisy. They would BANG! They would CRASH! They would SHOUT! until Dachy could hear nothing but NOISE!

HA HA! HO HO!

HEE! HEE!

HELLO!

One day, Dachy's friends were being particularly noisy. Emmy and Steggie were laughing loudly and Rex kept shouting too close to Dachy's ears.

Not wanting to spoil their fun, Dachy flew off for a rest. He turned off his hearing aid and sat down on a rock for a rest and some peace and quiet.

But it wasn't a rock! It was a very large, rather grumpy, Turtle. "Get off!" grumbled the Turtle rudely. But Dachy couldn't hear him. "I said, GET OFF!" the Turtle shouted crossly.

Dachy did not hear the Turtle. He did not move.
Dachy had fallen asleep! He then began to snore
very loudly! The grumpy Turtle was very cross.
He wandered off towards the river to get a drink.

As the grumpy Turtle knelt to drink the water, Dachy slid off his shell and landed on a passing log. Still fast asleep, Dachy began to float slowly downstream.

Rex, Emmy and Steggie noticed Dachy had disappeared and were looking for him. They had reached the riverbank when Emmy suddenly spotted Dachy. "Oh my goodness, look!" she cried.

Dachy was heading for a waterfall...
and at the bottom of the waterfall
was a very hungry looking alligator.

"DACHY, WAKE UP!" they all shouted. "Oh no!"
cried Rex, realising that Dachy couldn't hear them.
Rex had a plan. "Come on, everyone. Follow me!"
he called, and ran off as fast as he could.

They stopped at the edge of the riverbank, a little bit ahead of Dachy. Rex grabbed a tree branch and clambered onto Emmy's long neck. Emmy stretched out as far as she could across the water. With the long stick, Rex prodded Dachy awake.

Dachy jolted up and flew into the air just before the log tumbled over the waterfall and into the mouth of the alligator.

Aargh, ALLIGATOR!!

Dachy landed on the riverbank and turned his
hearing aid back on. "Oh my goodness, how
did I get here!" he said. "We're not exactly sure,"
Rex replied. "Why did you turn off your hearing
aid, Dachy?" asked Emmy with concern.

"Well I don't like it when you all shout. I can't
hear what anyone is saying," explained Dachy.
"Oh, Dachy, we're so sorry" they all agreed.
"We promise not to be so noisy next time we're playing."

"And I promise to let someone know where I'm going
if I want to be on my own next time," said Dachy.

As the friends headed back into the forest they all
listened quietly to the wonderful sounds all around them.
What sounds do you think they could hear in the forest?

Meet all the Dinosaur Friends - Steggie, Dachy, Rex and Emmy!

978 0 7502 7056 4

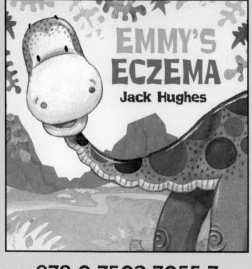

978 0 7502 7055 7

978 0 7502 7057 1

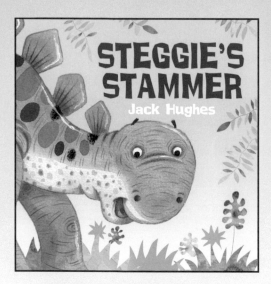

978 0 7502 7058 8